LOST REFLECTION

Dennis Callaci

BAMBOO
DART
PRESS

LOS ANGELES † NEW YORK † LONDON † MELBOURNE

Lost Reflection by Dennis Callaci

978-1-947240-68-1   Paperback

978-1-947240-69-8   eBook

Cover art by Dennis Callaci

Layout and design by Mark Givens

For information:

Bamboo Dart Press

chapbooks@bamboodartpress.com

Bamboo Dart Press 032

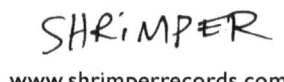

www.pelekinesis.com   www.bamboodartpress.com   www.shrimperrecords.com

Contents

Missing Reflection...5

We Have Always Been This Way.............................6

The Other Visitor...11

Two Deaf Zebras...26

All The Kings' Friends...31

32 Red...48

Richard and Manuel in The Hall of The Mountain King.............55

Joyful and Triumphant...65

Lost Reflection...69

Missing Reflection

Glass is missing in the door
I walk right in
I walk right in
No one stops me
I walk right in
I walk right in
I didn't kick it
I didn't ballbat it
I walk right in
I walk right in

The looking glass cloudy
The reflection went missing
I act like I belong here as I walk right in
I walk right in

We Have Always Been This Way

Gene had never held a baby before. Now, here he was on an Amtrak heading out to Sioux Falls holding some passenger's newborn. Who hands off a baby to a perfect stranger? I understand these are closed quarters and all, but I wouldn't entrust anyone on the rail bus with my wallet, not for a red-hot second, he thought. She was a single mom with a 4-year-old in tow (holding her sticky fingers up to show him as they attempted small talk when first boarding), along with the baby he was now holding. It was only for a few minutes, him all awkward-shouldered with the baby against his chest while the mother chased down the hollowed-out plastic ball that rolled a few rows up and engaged another, but it felt like days. Please don't cry, please don't die, please, not on my watch. Poor helpless thing. He thought about that wounded robin that he had shoe boxed with dirt, worms and leaves as a child. His father had air holed the cardboard. Didn't he know better? Was he just humoring me? My folks tucked me into sleep, they were a couple then, and when I awoke to find the poor thing lifeless in the morning, it was my mom that held me as I cried inconsolably. Please lady, get back here, beads starting to form all Jimmy Durante on my brow. "Thank you, thank you, sir, that was very kind of you," arms outstretched for the landing. "No problem, Ma'am," I said. It all felt very proper, military precision at play, was that even me? A version of me, a removed and unemotional façade that masked the panic that was playing out in my overactive mind anyway.

Spinning the day over later that eve, he would wonder why he had assumed that she was a single Mom. Because she was alone with two kids? No man to see her off at the station only what appeared to be her sister? Such a lack of imagination he told himself before quickly stealing a peak to see if she had a ring.

He had booked his ticket months ago for the evening to late morning. 8 pm to a pre-lunch station landing. Sleep was easy for Gene. Falling asleep to the white noise of the TV, on the couch to folks talking. He had taken this trip twice before over the last five years and had always been able to snatch a swath close to six hours of sleep. A baby bouncing on a knee, bassinet head bobbling, it wouldn't be too much further down these John Henry's until he was nodding.

Kids. Kids had broken up that relationship with Lydia. She wanted them, he didn't. Hell, I should have had one of these strangers snap a picture on my phone with that baby, and posted it with no explanation. Every ex likes to sleuth around where they shouldn't be. Come over here, to my page, to my post, to my domain. Maybe an ask will arise again before we get out of Ames. Too awkward to ask now and probably less so the closer he got to his sister's place. He kept thinking about the thread of this as he attempted sleep on that rented recliner. Not bad, he thought, as he settled in with a pillow for the small of his back. His sister, 2 years younger, had asked him to take this trek to visit her and her husband during his summer break. They made the haul to see me, the last two go rounds. Granted, this was easier as they had a car, but you can't expect a husband related only tenuously to you by law to make that drive repeatedly on his limited time off from work. This was a show of good faith, of my investment in our relationship. It was also to be my first-time home in years. My father and I have been estranged for over a decade. He had bad-mouthed me about something back then and it appeared to me that she was on his side. I beached them both as the weeks turned to years. We all dug in further. I don't think any of us were expecting that. Maybe dad. Sometimes time elapses and makes it more difficult to make an excuse over such minor grievances.

Phone call thaws over the last three years mended things with my sister and in turn, my brother-in-law who, excepting the endless conversations he must have endured, wasn't much invested in the whole of the thing. They have no children, my sister, and her husband, I wonder if that has something to do with our upbringing. Anything can be buried in the past, left to fend for itself. Why does it always surprise us, the bramble and weeds of it all that wildly grow back when we aren't looking?

-=-=-=-=-=-=-=-

The first thing that hit him when he awoke was how warm the left side of his face was. Section three of yesterday's newspaper pressure pushed against that window, the slow peel reveal as he stretched his arms and took stock of the company before him. 6:42 AM. There is of course no stop near Sioux Falls so I will be getting off at the closest station and continuing by bus for the remainder of the way. Some kind of snail trail slow-hub crawl with plenty of time to prepare myself. This too had been so long in the making that the actual order of the thing was missing details. It was the connecting line to his sister that had paved the way for this vacation free family reunion. This time was different with the added color of his father being present. There they would be picnicking out in the open air for all to see. Father, son & daughter with William as the aloof spectator, the nonblood line. Did he want kids? What must that conversation be like between the two of them? It was still on his mind, like fresh arguments that take days to fizzle and fade, these thoughts from the previous night.

"Thank you, mister, was nice talking to you." the mother says at 10:15 as we near. You can feel the anticipation in the cabin change, the pregnant stretch that is awaiting these fourteen-hour passengers. I wipe unseen crumbs from the thighs of my pant legs and say the same kind of inane things that I was trained to say, something like take care, or beautiful children, nothing you'd recount to anyone when you reach your destination. I have this credit card and phone as my compass and first aid. I will be the first responder, right there at the gate. We are meeting at The Falls Park Open Air Shelter. Neither dad nor the couple wanted to house all of us, I don't blame them. I am the baby; I am the only one that moved away. "What if something were to go wrong? This is just easier." my sister said for all of us. "After-wards you can stay with us, just don't mention it to dad. We'll play all of the aftermath by ear. Maybe you and he can take a walk together towards week's end, fish, I don't know what the two of you would you do, have a beer?"

The destination gets smaller the closer I get. "You are here" all red dotted in some kid's makeshift cab for the last leg. I ask the driver to stop at Skyway Liquor. I pause for a second thinking I should ask the kid if I can grab him anything. He is about five minutes away from never seeing me again, why bother? He probably doesn't want for anything, best to just get to where we are going without further delay. I grab a cold chardonnay for them, some Johnnie Walker Red, ice, and cups in case she hasn't thought of that. I pass on the miracle vitamins, power caffeine and crappy Lakota by China jewelry. They won't be needing anything else. I make my way out of the fanned door frame with a bag in each hand. The door slams with more force than I meant, I catch a look from the rearview and mumble an apology. We are driving through streets that used to know me. Avenues I bicycled with baseball cards in the spokes. I wipe my sweaty palms on my jeans. We make a left and I see them from a distance as we pull into the park. I grab the suitcase from the trunk and wrap the grocery bag handles around my right hand twice as I make it over to my family. I don't know why I agreed to come here. I don't know what to say. We have always been this way.

The Other Visitor

"*Margo? Margo?*" I am sitting with my palms under my thighs. I was listening but got lost somewhere five or so minutes back. One of the voices from the group brought me back from myself. It was my name spoken aloud. "Margo, may I introduce you or do you want to introduce yourself?" I blink twice and feel a jerk in the muscles in my legs. Quickly, I collect myself.

My first time, long time coming. Small talk. Short and void of details. She lets me leave it there after an awkward mid-sentence silence. I am thankful for mercy. I have always been nervous about speaking in public. Does this count as speaking in public? I don't know, but I am scared nonetheless. Sitting next to me on one of those tan packing tape-painted metal folding chairs is Derrick. I know him only because he introduced himself to me when we first sat down. "Been here two weeks. Welcome, Derrick." he said to me with just a few of us seated. His right arm bent at the joint up to his shoulder like one of those porcelain Maneki-Neko cats. Good fortune? Maybe. Maybe not.

-=-=-=-=-=-=-

If you were to see me, you would undoubtedly think that I am thirsty for attention. Tattoos rhymeless all over my body, brown eyebrows, bleached blonde hair with shocks of blue in it. Runway Rogue red lipstick. I am the one dressed up as the pretty male bird. I am the invisible chandelier overhead. The quiet, demure girl that was on the outskirts of your group of drinking pals. I want to be wallpaper here, but who is going to believe that? The act of coming here, even against your wishes, is a huge bouquet of attention.

-=-=-=-=-=-=-

The morning is one of them Best Western continental breakfast serve-yourself stations. No one is serving. I think of the armchair psychology that I know and apply it here. The coffee cups are small, girthy. The plastic utensils and paper plates sit on top of the microwave. Imagine yourself in space, I think, where an induced slumber of months has lifted. Scrambled eggs, half of a wheat bagel. I fumble the eggs onto the bagel only to scrape them off forgetting the pain of my jaw when I open too wide.

-=-=-=-=-=-=-

Third day in the circle. Eight people, four on my left and four on my right, a half-moon. Oh, I am the crown jewel in the ring when I am speaking, and I barely speak. On Thursday I hung my head and cried as Taran recounted history. It was one of them snot tear-spittle cries where your entire face is awash in a mix of it all. My head hangs with gravity pulling the tears out of me. She is here for a good reason. I cry for myself. I am not here for any reason at all. My history is a blank slim slate, tidy comparatively. Who can I blame that on? Boredom? It wasn't even experiment-ing that landed me here. Experimenting sounds so grandiose. I was just stalled and killing time. What is there to talk about?

I spend the next three histories working up what it is I am

going to say. I turn it over and over, polish and sand it. Pop quiz. Oral exam. Tell us something about you. I would have to unravel the entire yarn and dissect the pieces to find a proper beginning. It isn't worth it, unimportant, see, about that behind me. I don't have disdain for the past, or a need to erase it, I truly just don't see in it anything of worth in this present company. I wouldn't be here but for the future, but no one wants to talk about a future here. Seedless in a pod.

-=-=-=-=-=-=-

Derrick kicks my right shin. OW! Kicks my shin the way you slam a buzzing TV. That doesn't work on me, I am still all snowy. I slink and I slump. Move on to the next one. Move on to the next one. My body language could not be easier to read. The trick to it all is being quiet. Be small. When you creep down the hall and the floorboards alarm the occupants, curve your back, and hunch lower. Pretend not to hear them should their hollers trail you. It works wonders.

"I understand if you don't want to share Margo, your being here and listening is in fact sharing." It is the kindest thing I have heard in months. In months preceding this, I wasn't addressed all that much. Well, you have friends, you have family. I had one of those A-ha moments. 3:30 PM passed out on a lawn chair in the parking lot next to my car with caked vomit around my mouth and down my neck. A-ha! I wonder if that is what the girl scout mom and her daughter thought as I awakened to them nearly picking my lane to walk through and then backing up to the next pair of parked cars to skirt along. A brown cardboard box picked at fries and discarded lettuce tucked into the corner. It was just going to be a brief five minutes, feeling Ferris-wheely I bought a burger, then needed some air. I remembered the two beach chairs being in the trunk, the first to sit in and the second to put my legs up. A perfectly fine plan up until a few minutes after I retrieved them. Oh consciousness, you are so fucking high maintenance. I was all right then, no need to call in the Stater Bros., but someone please get a gurney of fabrics from JoAnne's Craft World. "We have a situation in the northernmost section of the parking lot." I can't start with that. My silence is not combative, I am just at a loss. The counselor, I think, sees that.

Derrick is next. He loves his turn as he campfire ghost stories us. His street pulpit prophet is a staple of these places, I imagine. The self-taught Buddhist. The wayward shepherd. Shhhh, sheep crossing. I am usually disdainful of his brand of school counseling, but here, it soothes me. He has not, as yet, tortured us with his sorrow. He is calm and removed, aloof not cool. I get most of the references he codes when speaking, but not today. "I am alright with feeling like the lesser version of the main attraction. The Knott's Berry Farm to Disneyland. At Knott's Berry Farm most of their rides are short, economic affairs that are built skyward because they have a lack of land. Disneyland is a sprawl. Rides can last ten, fifteen minutes. They have backstories & grandeur." Oh no, I bite my cheek. Another fucking parable on a parable about fairy tale fucking parables. "I don't have none of that. I feel like the EZ read version." He pauses and he stumbles for a second washing his left palm over the top of his right hand.

"There is this songwriter--was this songwriter, he's gone--named Daniel Johnston. He was from Texas. He recorded a song in the house that he shared with his mom which was a virtual cover of a Bruce Springsteen song. The Springsteen song is about Cadillac Ranch, a place where Cadillacs are buried vertically with four-fifths of their bodies exposed above the dirt, looking skyward. They look like a ride at Knott's Berry Farm. Rear window to the ground, steering wheel skyward. In the Daniel Johnston rewrite, he supplants Bruce's Cadillacs with coffins. Cadillac Ranch becomes a funeral home. His song is actually called Funeral Home." I like that, coffins instead of Cadillacs. I am unfamiliar with Daniel Johnston. I know who Bruce Springsteen is, but do I know any of his songs? I need to write down Daniel Johnston. I am going to forget. I can't remember the name of the faces around me that I have been living with for nearly a week. Most of them. I have to strain to remember the name of the therapist holding us at attention. Diane or Diana? Oh shit, it will come to me.

Is this what it feels like to be old? I am on the other side of Derrick today. I understand exactly what he is saying, but get none of the script of his touchstones. I think on this some more. I think about what it is and wonder. Derrick is going on "...clean three years and then" – POP - he slams his two hands together. The gaunt old dude next to Derrick rubs at his shoulder and back. I sit trying to look in between the two chairs of the visitors across from me. No one wants to make eye contact. My turn is coming some other day.

-=-=-=-=-=-=-

If I had a sharpie, I would have two pecks of five scrawled on the wall. Like tattoos, I would be embarrassed, and ashamed of them in mixed company, so maybe it is fifty-fifty. Maybe I would have them on the left-hand side of the bed to mark time, maybe not. Funeral home. Shame. We work our entire lives telling people our life story and then some ghostwriter punches up their version and it trumps all others. This is the closest I am going to come to a final version, for now.

"I am twenty-seven. I have spun aimlessly for a decade. Nothing accomplished, I mean nothing. Jack shit. I am still seventeen in my head. I am still undocumented, an unknown quantity even to myself. Arrested development. A runaway, nomad, rogue."

I sputter and my voice doesn't sound like my own. It is like Broadway singing, how that isn't singing at all. No one sings like that in real life. Opera. I wish Broadway was replaced with nothing but opera houses. Fuck your stupid live renditions of bad motion pictures. Go back to the classics. Spin. Spin. Spin. Quick, wash away the memory of what you just said and how you said it.

I look up. No one is crying, no one is doing much of anything. Bored pigeons at arms-length on a stoop waiting for me to leave so that the ground can be reclaimed.

-=-=-=-=-=-=-

It is the shape of a dial. I turn to see what the next song could be. It is Pete, fifty something, salt and pepper. No one is going to cry for you Pete. I heard you on Wednesday and Thursday. I have no control of the station. I can't find no on/off.

-=-=-=-=-=-=-

The sleeve of my sweater is frayed and I notice all of the pills along the bottom of my right arm on the material that need to be pulled. Would anyone here have one of them battery-operated QVC jobbies that you run along the course fabric to cut at them and get them off? It is a battle of will to not pick at them on my first one-on-one. Diane/Diana wears business cool teal, a white satin shirt, and an out-of-place wood beaded necklace, orange.

My nails are chewed down, I trace along the cross tattoo between my forefinger and my thumb as she preambles. Diane/Diana, I am sorry, for I have nothing of note to say.

"Margo, you don't have to-"

I wait, thinking there is an ellipsis...

-=-=-=-=-=-=-

MARS

JUPITER

SATURN

The gurgle of a transmission "KELLER-17866-KELLER-ARRIVAL TIME 21:36". In my head, the mantra. I turn to one side, feel a stretch and pull as I do so. I open my eyes to a perforated screen. Like a silver screen, but white, enamel, plastic? Vaseline weighing my lids down. Right, right. There is motion as the vacu-seal of the temporary coffin lifts. It elevates in that slow arm electronic manner that has always troubled me. No whirr, but it worries me that were there a malfunction, I would not be able to manually open it from inside. Hell, I've no strength to even lift my legs right now.

"Keller"

"KELLER"

It is Morgan. My throat all razor dry and unforgiving. I can't eke out a sound. I try to move my arm or my lids or my leg as a way of response. He puts a warm compress over my eyes.

"Give it ten minutes. You might feel nauseous, but you won't vomit. I am going to survey the rest of the crew. You remember the drill, first one up makes the coffee." He laughs.

I am gauzy, not nauseous. I hear Taran, her voice booming as she shares a laugh with Morgan -well, paints over his laughter with hers more so than sharing. I am able to slowly sit up. Morgan winds back over "Hey, hey, hey, take it easy there. Your body needs to get acclimated, lay back down there Boudicca." He had called me that for nearly as long as I had known him. It didn't quite endear me to him, the pretentiousness of it, but it beat the hell out of Xena.

I slowly ease down which seems more difficult and less possible than the act of sitting up. I feel it in my head as I search for it to land. How far down do I need to go to land? I hear others stirring, I start to feel a pain that extends from my right ear into my jaw. I wonder if my teeth grinding bypassed the anesthetic. It feels like an ear infection followed by the pulsing of a fresh upper cut. The laying back down is indeterminable as I veer in and out of those quick pre wake dreams.

I am in the old house. I walk down the hall and turn left into the first of three bedrooms. My folks' room. I notice what looks like the ghost frame of a painting that had hung for years and appears to have been taken down recently. A horizontal rectangle, five by three foot in size. I get closer. I notice a seam split running down the middle of it, a draft coming through. I push on the wall. There is a click as the wall becomes a door. I peer in, it is my dad but it isn't my dad. He is painting. "Margo, either come in or close the door." I swallow into a coughing fit. Morgan hovers above me as I awaken. I steady myself gripping his arm as I sit up and then stand.

-=-=-=-=-=-=-

"I do not advise that we go off of trajectory. It will cost us too much time and risk the fruitfulness of the mission." Capt. D. Silver it reads on her lapel. We have run into a shower of dead meteors and though we suffered minor damage, there are two spherical rings between us and Saturn. "We can get through that, we already got through one." says Taran. I say nothing.

We are having a communal meal, only our third since we came out of hibernation. Reconstituted eggs. Reconstituted juice. Tempers should not be flaring. We are a seasoned crew and seven out of eight of us have worked together before. Unfortunately, the Captain makes eight.

I insert myself into the silent tension. "Couldn't we wait and take another forecast as we draw closer? The coordinates indicate that we are still two hundred plus hours from the next shower. There is a solid chance that the shower will dissipate or be knocked off course before we near it, at least the one we first approach. The second one is nearer to Saturn and with the force of it, is likely to remain."

Silver sits stoic, her eyes steely. After an indeterminable three minutes, she is the next to speak. "I agree with moving forward with Keller's plan. There is the possibility that the axis of the sphere shifts or that we time our entry in such a way as to avoid the majority of meteorites through the final arc." I nod, look to my left and right, but the other six crewmates are being certain not to approve or nod knowingly. The responsibility will lie on our shoulders. Diane/Diana and Margo.

-=-=-=-=-=-=-

I open the half door. It pops with the push and then clicks automatically from the hinges. My father is standing, facing north. He has a glass of water on a barstool to the left of him. No ice. He sees me, but says nothing. I don't dare enter. I don't want to disturb anything. I think, upon waking, this could have been the saddest stand-up comedy act I have ever seen.

-=-=-=-=-=-=-

Derrick is in the kitchen, washing dishes. I hear it through the near cardboard of our bedroom door that he has shut. He is telling Roselynn to keep quiet. "Sh, sh, shhhh. Mommy is resting. You don't want to rest right? You don't want a nap. So, let's be quiet and you can stay up for as long as she naps."

We went back and forth on what the last name of our child would be. He didn't take my name, and I didn't take his. *Margo Morgan?* Sounds like a bad smoothie or a show and tell zoo orangutan. Rose for his mom, Lynn for mine. No hyphened name but her middle name is mine. Roselynn Keller Morgan. It has lost some of its initial impression now that she is here. Before she was born, I thought with a name like that, it was going to be a law firm that crawled out of me.

I have a habit of falling asleep with the TV on. I mean, I do it purposely, but it is not something that Derrick took too. So, most nights the TV is off as we fall into slumber, but naps, my naps, I leave that sucker on. I love the intersection of where my consciousness starts to blur and when I segue from whatever is on into an under-colored, ill-defined tread of whatever it is my sleeping mind wants to exorcise. Antonioni's *Red Desert* into me alone on a beach walking a railroad track for miles as it stretches but a few feet from the shore. The waves lap at my ankles, splash on my shins as the tide comes in. The court TV case about the pampered dog that turned into a requiem for an ugly duckling prom queen.

I turn to my left side with a pillow between my knees, then to my back with the pillow on my belly.

-=-=-=-=-=-=-

There is no one as alone as the former lover. Not a lover that is spurned, or red hot dropped, but the lover that is forgotten. The lover that is supplanted by a sickness that mines the memory banks, pumps fool's gold hollow reality into the consciousness and makes not only the victim merely a visitor but the entire orbit of souls around her phantom energy, strangers. Well, we two are both victims. You, you with selective recall and me here now holding court with all of our memories as a service in real time for you.

BANG! They had to restrain you on a visit months back, onto a gurney, then clicked into the bed.

-=-=-=-=-=-=-

"Happy fourteenth birthday" Dad says to me, subtly ironic given things. He drops me off and this morning I think about where he is headed to. He stopped recounting how she is doing, or what the nurses said or what the prognosis was a good while ago. He tells me that it is better if I don't go, this after he pried out of me some time ago that it hurts me far too much to go than to be away. I read manga; I skirt around rabbit holes all night skipping from footage of shark attacks to cheat codes to the next level of *Pirate Coven*.

"Wow, must be cool to have a swimming pool." Arthur says first time over to my house.

"Yeah, cooler than having a vegetable Mom."

That shuts him right up.

-=-=-=-=-=-=-

His hand over her hand, then under her hand, then pushing on the bar of the bed, then mapping out a way to lift his coat over the ribbon of the drip to kiss her brow.

-=-=-=-=-=-=-

He brings a flask with him. It is filled with cream. It makes the longer days bearable. The coffee is okay, but he learned long ago not to opt for it with milk out of the vending machine as it makes the coffee altogether too sweet. He likes some bite in his drink, which makes the entire concept of a flask filled with cream hilarious to him. But there he is, three cups in at a quarter after five PM, pouring the last of it into one of them small wide coffee cups. The sound of his voice, to her, it might slide in. It might marry to whatever secret activity is going on inside of there. He narrates his actions to her. The poor roommates he has seen come and go. They have no choice. He stopped asking after the third one said no, he would prefer if Derrick would not speak.

"One more for the road, honey." Flask up heavenward, just above his right shoulder.

-=-=-=-=-=-=-

The shine of the waxed linoleum in the hallway and the blur of tears in my eyes soft focuses things, an aura of one of those documentaries about out of body experiences. The valleys on screen have flattened out and the help has rushed in to blunt the loop of death. Unplug the EKG. Unclasp the fingertip pulse line. They had been forecasting this for days.

"Mr. Morgan, I am so sorry." One of the Rounds folk that I knew best says as I leave the room and the yellow curtain is drawn along the glass in the control room. The help are all at their stations, monitoring other landings. Dazed, I push the metal bar on the door of the ward, pass two middle aged women in gowns, make up. I take the first right, the one I took a dozen times in the last few days, and find a wall in the hallway away from everyone.

I hesitate, but then call Roselynn who is en route to get here. She doesn't pick up, for the best, I'll tell her when she arrives. I call my sister. I ask her to make the other round of calls.

"Can you do me a favor though, wait an hour? I haven't told Roselynn, I haven't told anyone, I want her to hear it from me, not on a screen."

"Oh Derrick, of course, of course. Whatever you need." Then a crack in her voice as she softly closes, "Just let me know if there is anything I can do."

I breathe an "okay" into the phone, looking up at the fluorescent lights as if they can absorb the edge of my grief.

Where do I go. Do I stay here? Do I wait in her room with her? The hallway, parking lot? An answer as I peer into her room and see two white coated figures addressing the body. I get into my car and arrive home without remembering if I ran any lights.

-=-=-=-=-=-=-

I put my keys and wallet on the kitchen counter. Restack the mail that is there into a tighter stack after a quick flip before heading into the front parlor. Two teak wood chairs, recently redone for us as an anniversary gift. She would sit in the Easternmost one. Sleep on her side, me on my back. Our heads to the north, her on the west, me on the east. It didn't matter which way you were facing. East is east. I sit in her chair. I face north. A stack of newspapers slouch on the hearth of the fireplace. Our house, it is dressed up as it was when it awaited our return from vacations. Awaiting some heat or A/C.

The caterers are outside clothing the tables, arranging dessert trays, getting drinks on ice. I see two of them through the slider sharing a smoke. You would love that and I am more than happy to give the allowance to them to stub their cigarettes out on the lawn. I pace the house some more and wait. Prepare myself. I know I will do better in company. It is the preshow jitters. It is the loose stool, dry mouth, heart in chest act all for naught. The show is over. Everything has already happened.

My index and middle right fingers are glued together, tapping on my temple, nervously, thoughtlessly. I don't look up, but straight down the hallway. The bathroom door is open and I can make out my darkened figure in the mirror. We are here only to grow lesser in time. To look unlike ourselves. Writers who can no longer read. Ballplayers that can't follow the game. A shadow curtains the light of the front door, then the soft knock of the first arrival.

Two Deaf Zebras

He was one of those. The guy at the party you desperately try to get away from. The one telling endless strings of unfunny jokes. Worse than his jokes and his physical presence was his laugh. His laugh punctuating each joke, often before the punchline. HAHA... haheh, in a register two octaves up from his speaking voice. Ratty.

We were thrown together to clean up a mess. It was a fucking mess alright. HAHA... haheh, looking over at me for a read. I figured it best to not submit. Issue nothing to his setups and punchlines. No side eye, no grimace, nothing in either direction. Keep cool. Stay calm. I was already in enough trouble. Trouble got me in this place and then sunk me lower into this kind of duty on account of bad behavior. You have to act. You have to lash out soon upon entry, take your lumps at the get-go instead of for the duration.

"Did you hear about the whore from Pensacola?"

"Her name was Bubbles, found her in the Hudson, she sank. HAHA..." trail off.

The logic is skewed and doesn't make sense. *Bubbles?* No, Bubbles would have floated back up to the surface. Pensacola? The entirety of it was off.

This was another of my sentencings delivered to serve as penance for those that I hurt, crimes I had committed. Atonement, for the scales of justice to live vicariously through me. This one was for soliciting. You can sell your soul out, but watch out what you do with your body. It taught me the value of each.

My heel sends my body on a quick second slide, the viscosity of the oil on these cheap-issue tennis shoes. I catch with arms out akimbo, imagine myself as a child learning to skate. Shaky. I was so shaky and frightened that first time. That first crime. Eleven. Stop N' Go. Pulled a knife and took the register drawer with a stack on top, my hands sandwiching it so I could deadweight the loose bills into Gage's car without losing any of it. I was under-armed. That was Gage's idea.

"You gotta do this with your gut, not a gun."

Must be what hazing feels like, those entryways. The knowing smiles in the Oldsmobile, knee slap about the clerk's facial expression at seeing a kid that hasn't even hit puberty coming at him with a knife. "You might find some hair there overnight!" Gage says to me while he and his pal laugh cigarette smoke out the windows.

I knew the guy across the counter from dozens of transactions. I wasn't scared. I acted on my feet and had a backup plan that Gage and his pals were unaware of. They could see me through the glass but couldn't hear me. I pointed my left forefinger at the clerk with direction and with my right hand pointed my blade to the parking lot "I got armed pals in that waiting car, don't fuck with me." Of course, he recognized me. Caught the car's plates and netted me a few days later. I was new under wing, little greenie with a blade. That was my first armed robbery. My first failure then.

I am back from the business, back in the company of the inmates. I know some of them. That happens on repeated returns. I am one of those turnstilers. Miserable bastards, most of them. I got landed because of the company I kept, things that I knew. They wanted a plea deal, to pump me for details on acquaintances. I wanted worse to return to my neighborhood again and walk freely. This was going to be a quick bounce anyway. If you open yourself up to their offers of spring, you'll end up dead-ended in some alley. I took the rap and kept my mouth shut repeatedly. After that first sentencing, it was Vincent, not Gage, that told me "Look straight ahead, but if it becomes insurmountable, look at your shoes like you do when you walk them steep hills. It is elementary school easy. Keep your nose clean and mind your own biz."

What a joke, employing that all these years later with a dude that I could crush in a second. He prattles on and on. I try to dig down deeper into thought, recount memorized lyrics or stories. A silent book report. I had gotten into the practice of writing. Writing fiction, non-fiction, short stories in my mind. Editing and laboring over these pieces the way mechanics open-heart cars. Find the right fit, perfect the greasy underbelly and tame the beast of the thing. Turning it over in my mind repeatedly. The good ones stuck. The good ones got *Roget's Thesaurus*. Oh, the rib I would take on the outside. Dumb junkie whore writing poetry, still cheating.

"Two deaf zebras walk into a bar..."

Waltz into a bar, I thought. Waltz. That would be funnier.

There is glass everywhere. Soda pop gurgle tar that smears onto everything. There is no getting this slop up.

We pour sand on the sludge. Ten-pound bags. Sand on the glass. We are surgeons sent into an OR with toothpicks. I wonder through the hum of noise. I think about possible endings. There is no good outcome. Slightly better outcomes, sure, but not a good one comes to mind. Rubbing the rouge into the red, the ocean into the sea, the asphalt blending with tar. "HAHAHA, get it? You don't get it do you?" I try to get back into myself, work twice as hard as him to soften the offense that he is taking from my silence. I don't want to talk. No small talk. I get nothing from it but exhausted.

In the fifth grade, I read a book about a child killer. A cheap paperback that belonged to my dad. I got lost as his character described in verse picking a lock. Disarming his victim. I had to go back, back to where he said he was scared of the dark, made himself appear frail, human in an earlier chapter. It was the first time that literature spoke to me. That I understood simile, metaphor, and iconography. I don't remember the author's name or the book title, but that chapter stuck with me.

The little girl in the novel, the main character, outwits the killer. She would have been the fourth victim, but she isn't. It was above my station as a ten-year-old, but still, I understood the thrust of it. It was not some *Boys from Brazil* abstraction that I read soon thereafter but did not retain. This was cheap psychology. Her escape was pure paint by number, but at that time, new to me. Play opossum. Agree with your captives. Don't speak or plead, as that way, what you do say will hold more water.

She says, "I am glad I am not alone right now, tonight. I would be so scared." She can see his guard is down as he lowers his eyes and then looks up at the ceiling. Gritty knees up off of the pavement as she makes like she is going to sit next to him. She kicks him square in the groin, and bat hells it out of the basement.

It had quieted down. We can see that we are getting to it, that save for another job of the same makeup, there will be a respite soon. It must be past noon. I can feel my back starting to seize up from shoveling. I can go a bit longer, but not much. We switch me with the empty bags, then me with the bagged dregs. If we can finish this one, we won't have another tomorrow. I imagine that this is a workout, that I am in training. I pretend that I am a method actor, then a research psychologist. The trick to staying sane is playing games, imagining.

I am two bags behind. I bring the first to my bent knee. The burlap is splitting as I attempt to right leg lift with it, the sludge pours down my left leg, down my calf, some spilling into my shoe. The joker is not amused, he is sputtering at me as the slush claims more ground. All lowercase and pithy "fuck, fuck, fuck." I slide up and begin again. Two deaf zebras waltz into a bar.

All The Kings' Friends

MARCO

Jerry King had already died by the time I got to him. My second call rang and rang before an AI message relayed that voice mail had not been set up by the user. I arrived pushing the digits to his place to be let in. The buzz went unanswered. Call 911? Maybe he is in the shower? Calm down, calm down just wait one moment. It is a simple thing, wait slightly out of view, or even near view walking just a few steps behind an entering renter, and you are in. Okay, okay, here is a first-chance entry. Shuffling with my phone and acting preoccupied, I grabbed the wrought iron gate by the top lip as an elderly couple exited. Act as though I know the place like the back of hand and those rushing by will pay no mind. These gated apartment communities are never as secure as most of the tenants believe them to be. It had been a gurgle of a call, but he said he needed a ride. He didn't think he could drive to the nearest urgent care, sweat fever, weakened. He had to be all right I thought to myself.

He had really been something in his youth, a provocateur, a man of ideas. He was well-loved in the weirdo community that he fell into. Painters, writers, folks that rented airplane hangars in Banning, California to reside in. Hot plates and space heaters to stay warm during them freezing edge of the desert Southern California nights. That youth, his youth well past middle age, did not translate into wealth was not of concern to him. "I never even thought about it until I was in my early sixties." He had said to me a few years back. "Retire? Retire on what? To do what?"

"I have no kids, no caretakers, no close family and no savings. I gotta just put my faith in the wind." He smiled and let rip a fart that made it clear in that greasy spoon that not one of the patrons inhabiting the place was an actor. He had a fart on deck and wanted to make the most of it. What the hell else good are farts anyway? Punctuation. The funniest punctuation mark ever created. "Suck on that Laurence Olivier!" he was fond of saying.

His ex-wife was still friendly with him. And he had, what I thought, were a lot of close friends. He didn't need the wind. The motley crew of us would serve to see that he got his meds, take him to doctor appointments should he suffer from a broken hip, take shifts should a malady should arise and he needed watching. He didn't have to think about loose ends or unkempt end-of-life plans.

Over time our friendship, like all well-built friendships, changed. Ten years his junior, it was not a large enough gap in age to see-saw us. My youth to his wisdom, nothing like that. I corrected him, disagreed liberally with him, told him he had an errant ear hair or a mustard stain on his chin from the day before, the kind of shit you wouldn't say to a boss or an uncle. I also dug. I asked questions about something I heard or read about him, not psychosycophant style, but not far from the realm of what and how you might ask a far-limbed family member about your grandfather or your ma when she was young.

I was due to be at his apartment later that day anyway. I had scored a bootleg cut of one of a myriad of half-finished Orson

Welles films we were going to view together. I had sat on it for weeks but waited so that my first viewing would be Jerry's first viewing. John Huston, Susan Strasberg.

With our lifetime of experience, neither one of us had ever been within a twenty-five-foot pole of working on a movie. Not a gopher, a script doctor, an extra, or a paper pusher exec, but that did not bar us from our love nor understanding of what makes a film tick. I remember putting the paper-thin Amaray case on the pass-through as I entered his place calling out "Jerry...Jerry... JERRY."

Just off of the turn of his ratty old couch I saw his lower third, thighs to sole laying prone. He was covered in a pool of sweat, not moving or nodding as my voice rose in concert with my shaking of his mid-section, belly up. After the phone calls, the ambulance, the gawkers and the confusion of what seemed like hours, I was alone in his place. Do I lock his door once they take his body? Does he have his keys? Do I search for his keys? I was thinking about anything other than what I knew then. Didn't need no EMT. No ENT either. Jerry was gone, he had left the fucking building before I set foot in it.

"Your relation to him?"

"What kind of medication does he take?"

"Was he conscious when you got here?" and more questions before they drove off with him.

"St. Luke's." and other answers before I was alone in his apartment.

I find an address book by his landline. How recent was the last entry? Well, hell, I had an old one lying around my house and hadn't put an entry into it in twenty plus years, but some of those names & numbers were still good. We had a few shared old friends, but I don't know if I had any contact information for one of them. I grabbed the book before spinning the inside lock of the knob & shutting the door.

I put a call into St. Luke's, there was not a need to come down. Did I have the contact for any immediate family members? the attendant on the phone asked. "I dunno, I might have, can I call you back?" I said in the stupor that I had been in since the afternoon. I poured a single malt into a glass, neat. I remember when I first started drinking scotch, ordering it clean instead of neat. I would have liked to have told Jerry that, as I sat in the armchair facing the vent in the front den. The cold air hit me. The night is mercifully quiet on one of them eves where every backyard A/C unit spins and hums its masters to sleep.

-=-=-=-=-=-=-=-=-

I asked for a table for ten. The hostess asked if the entire party was present. I had guessed ten, as I didn't know how many of us would be showing up. "No, just the two of us right now."

"Let me know when the entire party is here and we will seat you then," she said, turning to a server to say something. I cut her off, "Make it a party of two and seat us then." She gave me the look of one who takes any veering from some imaginary laundry list as an affront. "Two, please", I said.

"You can sit at the bar and have a drink until the remainder of your party arrives." She is saying this to me in that "guest" as opposed to "customer" tone of voice which raises my ire.

"No, table for two."

"Marco, let's wait, even just ten minutes," Wendy says.

"Two." I ignore Wendy and now both the hostess and Wendy are on the same side, subtle contempt as we are led to a table for two.

"I miss the smoking section..." Wendy says as we walk towards the back of The Lemon Tree which has changed hands at least three times in the years that we have been frequenting it.

"...in airplanes, even on fucking sidewalks."Wendy moves her chair up against the wall, owl eyeing the plinth that the hostess preens behind. She is not side-eyeing the hostess, which I have already done, but keeping a watch on who comes into the restaurant.

"Shirley, over here!" Wendy waves her in.

Big Shirley. She is, was, a friend of Jerry's that both Wendy and I know. She walks towards a table for two, with two chairs, pulls a chair from the empty table for four next door, and sits at what I suppose is the head of the table – unless you count the wall where the other would-be table setting is.

"Oh Marco, I am so sorry that you were the one to find him."

Big Shirley says this because not only is she an RN, but her current gig is as a hospice nurse.

"I have seen dead before, Shirley, and he was dead when I got there. There was nothing that anyone could have done, I mean, besides what you are doing now."

Shirley had taken the baton as she knew more of his current inner circle and made the round of phone calls, telling us to meet here.

"I did get in touch with his sister," Shirley says as she adjusts the strap of her purse against the retro vinyl backing of her chair.

"Excuse me miss," the waitress arriving with two glasses of water says as she slides the sweaty glasses to each of us. "We need to keep this aisle open as per the fire codes. I can move you to this table." She motions at the table for four next to us.

"Sure, no problem," Shirley says, getting up and moving her chair to its rightful space.

"I told you Marco, and what are you going to do when more people arrive?" Wendy says more than truly asking.

"Well, we can move that table for two next to this one, and viola, we have room for six, hell maybe eight if the fire codes allow."

I am pissy. I can't change gears midstream right now.

"You are such an impossible asshole sometimes, I swear," Wendy says.

"Better an impossible asshole than a real one." Shirley cracks, trying to defuse things.

"...Anyway, I talked to Louise-" Wendy interrupts Shirley, "Who is Louise?"

"Louise is Jerry's older sister. She lives outside of Vegas. Said she hadn't talked to Jerry in a stretch."

"I had no idea he had any living family, never said anything to me about no Louise." I play with the ear of the menu where the laminate is splitting.

Shirley continues, "I met her once. Jerry and I went to Vegas, I don't know, a decade, fifteen years ago to catch Don Rickles at The Orleans. She was straight, a small talker. You know, moaning about a neighbor, bitching about the crap install of some wood flooring. She was so not Jerry."

"Can I get you started with drinks?" the waitress says on her return.

"Iced tea for me," says, Wendy.

"Coffee, black please."

"Could I get a glass of ice water?" Big Shirley says.

"Anything else with that?" the waitress says as though she is moving mountains, trying to get that extra quarter and dime for their tip with add-ons and sides.

"That'll do hon, thanks." Shirley dismisses her kindly.

A huge booming, stretched out "HHHHHEEEEYYYYYY!" as Reggie rounds the table to sit next to me.

Reggie, I met him through Jerry. Reggie looks exactly like a Reggie, only now, older. Must be six three, 250 pounds, dimple chin, and a strutting gait when he walks. He is super friendly; I mean to a fault. Kind to the undeserving.

You might think it odd, given the circumstances, that Reggie would make an entry like he was celebrating a friend's birthday here just a few days out from Jerry's death, but damn, his levity is appreciated now more than ever by me. Some folks just don't get down. Maybe Reggie's being a Jehovah's Witness has something to do with his stellar disposition. I don't know. He gets his salvation when he is dead, knowing that, death means release and happiness for him. We have talked about everything at one point or another I think to myself. Is this new territory? Jerry's death? We have danced around religion and politics and sports and brassieres. "Why don't they make them pointy bras like they did in the fifties? Not that Ariana Grande double dunce ice cream cone cup, but like what the dames wore in those noir films?" he asked me once.

Jerry was an apostate. A former Jehovah's Witness himself, he had joked with Reggie in my presence about what a load of hooey he thought it all was. "No Christmas presents for you Reggie, that is what I like about you." He would joke, substituting the birthday in place of Christmas as we drew closer to July 15th, Reggie's birthday. I remember the date as he shared the same birthday as my former anniversary. A fair trade, subbing his birthday in place of that mistake of a marriage.

"Jerry is not in heaven, Reggie, why are you so smiley?" Big Shirley calmly greets him.

"Oh, he will be forgiven, and he will go to heaven Shirley." Her face is a tell. My turn to redirect the boat.

"Did you know that Jerry had an older sister Reggie?" I ask while our drinks are placed before us.

"Is this your entire party?" The waitress asks.

"Yes," I say over a "No" papered over by Wendy.

Are you trying to trick question me, Brenda, if your name tag can be believed? A fly at the funeral. Maybe if I told her that we were mourning the death of our friend she would back off and cool her shit.

"Yes, this is it for now," Shirley confirms.

"How about I get your drink order sir and then take your orders on my return." She says to Reggie, and in turn, us.

"I'll have a water and a coffee with cream and sugar."

There is cream and sugar on the table. She brought the cream and sugar when she brought my black coffee. No one listens. No one is observant. There is a silver creamer and a cracked enamel sachet holding the real and fake sugars right smack in the middle of the table. I suppose if both read and believed what I read in the Watchtower that I would be able to easily overlook this and the hundreds of other things that drive me crazy on a weekly basis. Nonetheless, I forgive Reggie, just as God forgives Jerry.

"Louise, God, I haven't seen her in years, is she still alive?" Reggie asks me.

"Well, according to Shirley she is." my hand motioning to Shirley.

"Yes, she is alive. She is flying into Ontario on Wednesday. She is going to be down here for a week to clean up Jerry's things. The service won't be for a number of weeks as she wants to get whatever there is of an estate in order, she says it is a mess."

"Ha, and of course it is!" Wendy laughs.

"What kind of estate are we talking about? You mean, cardboard boxes of old ratty ass pulp paperbacks, VHS tapes of old movies, and a wardrobe consisting of five costume changes?" Reggie cracks.

The food is ordered, arrives, and is mostly devoured over a half hour. There are no further issues over the course of the meal as no one else arrives, orders or eats. Just the four of us, pals of Louise's little brother. I throw an extra ten on top of the scattered ones for the tip. I'll show Brenda. Be kind to people. Bend the rules now and again, no one cares about trite small things.

-=-=-=-=-=-=-

WENDY

She and Marco had been on-again, off-again lovers, at the tail end of on-again right now, suspended in what would have been over had Jerry not died. This week served as a gentle end. Her being here and simultaneously making herself less present for him. A magic trick like when you give notice to your workplace but can't disappear fast enough. Can't I just leave right now, right now? She thought.

Alone, she rolls over to the left-hand side of the bed. The ashtray on the dresser waiting for her to put the phone face down on the comforter, kick off her shoes and exhale toward the curtained windows. Soon she will fall asleep, bathed by the blasting of the A/C. In the morning she will warm up what amounts to three-quarters of a cup of coffee from yesterday's pot, relieved to be heading home the day after next.

-=-=-=-=-=-=-=-

REGGIE

He wasn't always a Jehovah's Witness. Raised Lutheran, he had converted five years ago. It was a sit down with each friend for which he felt as though he was put upon. He had done nothing wrong and now had to confess to his closest friends, most of them agnostic or lapsed in whatever denomination they may have belonged to. "It is not a cult, and furthermore it has absolutely nothing to do with you or our friendship." He told one soon-to-be ex-friend.

His family had grown to accept his faith, but could not get past the no-gift exchanging plank. "I just feel awful pulling out a trunk of presents on Christmas and not having one for you." His older brother told him. What could Reggie do? He would tear into them packages and found that last Christmas he had no guilt about his lack of gifting anything to anyone. It was fucking heavenly he would tell his friends if only he could bring himself to say such out loud.

It is the small things that you miss when you are alone. He had been alone for over a decade. Not a date in the teeth of nearly all of his twenties. This weekend was not going to end his losing streak, that was not even on his mind when he invited Mika to stay over, but it was nice to have a woman in his place, if even just for the sake of her convenience and the low-rent conversation of what might just be passing ships.

"Michelle's house is too small. Two kids, the indoor dog, and Peter, whom you know I hate, eat up all of the real estate." She told Reggie over the phone earlier that week. He offered her the couch for the weekend, and she jumped. "Oh, a couch in your front room? I would take the bathtub instead of Michelle's place! Check me in!" she laughed. She had flown in from Rochester for the service. Jerry was Mika's friend. Michelle only knew him in passing because of her sister, so it made more sense for her to stay with Reggie instead anyway. Plus, she and Reggie could tag along together over the weekend as, besides the service, there would be meals with their pals and an evening of drinks that was planned at Gato Negro.

-=-=-=-=-=-=-

BIG SHIRLEY

Big Shirley was five foot four, a hundred and sixteen pounds and loud as hell. Now in her late fifties, she had put on a few pounds since I first met her, but was untouched by time otherwise. I thought she was an ex-wife of Jerry's when we met, but now I know that she could not have been more than an ex-girlfriend. Even after years of the conversation turning to Jerry and Shirley's relationship at one or another of our places when the two of them were absent, or over cheap drinks, none of us had the foggiest. Shirley would always say that the two of them were just friends. Jerry intimated more on several occasions.

"Big Shirley? Jerry nicknamed me that. It was early in our friendship and he said he already had a friend named Shirley. I said, so what, I know people named Jerry, I ain't holding that against you! He laughed, started calling me Big Shirley, and then over time lost the Shirley and came to just calling me Big for Big

B, which I guess was short for Big Big?" she is laughing with tears in her eyes in the parking lot of the church as we gather. None of us wanting to go into the church.

"Reggie, is this place Lutheran or Mormon or what?" Shirley asks.

"I predict that it is prepaid and that it is cheap to rent," says Reggie, refusing to take offense of any kind.

"It looks like a fucking UFO made out of concrete, so I know it isn't Catholic." As she flicks her cigarette against the door of some poor fool's Honda compact, she reaches through Reggie to give me a hug.

"Oh, right, because Catholics don't need flight to get them to the heavens." I quip.

There is great comfort in taking the vinegar out of your friends and family on these occasions when you all are enveloped with sorrow. The great blanket of sadness that wraps around us gives way to these odd farewells in temples or graveyards that we will never visit again. We choose not to gather anywhere that houses joy for these funerals. We want to keep these goodbyes contained in faraway places that hopefully most of us will never see again.

"Right Marco, damn straight!"

The service needn't happen, and there is no reason for a reception afterward. We are, all of those that I know that are attending, saying our goodbyes to Jerry in this parking lot. Saying our goodbyes to one another with promises of a shared bottle of wine once we return to the rhythm of our regular lives. Of course, we won't do that until one or the other of us is missing at the next gala this size minus one.

"I never, ever go to hospitals if I can help it, but I don't mind funerals, I don't know why," Wendy says.

"I have a thing for the hard wooden pews and the formality of it all. It is like time traveling, rewinding. Who would want to sit in there, why?"

"Hmm, maybe people of faith Wendy?" I say half joking.

"No, I mean seriously, who here is a person of faith that you know other than Reg, and what are they all thinking at these services outside of their sadness? Like, we are supposed to take up communion and be scared shitless because death is super real for us at this moment in time? It is just so weird."

"Well, that is a real downer." Shirley laughs. I can see that Wendy feels rebuffed by this, this not being taken seriously.

"At least at burials, there is no ask of the loved ones gathered to repent and embrace God. It just seems needy and inappropriate."

"Well," Reggie quickly slides in, "Maybe we will escape that fate today. Maybe the officiant isn't from the church, right? I think Jerry's sister is going to adhere to his wishes. The dude wanted to be buried, not cremated, and wanted a service in a church for whatever reason."

"It is just weird," Wendy says quietly.

-=-=-=-=-=-=-=-

I am rolling Mika's sweaty shirt up over her back, we are crashing into each other. It is not romantic or animal, it is a mess of a

44

rush at her sister's place. Michelle is going to take her to the airport early tomorrow morning, and after dropping Mika off, she invited me in. "The family is out; they are at a fucking Angels game." Small talk, then a hug goodbye which she advanced on. The little dog is jumping up and down on our legs, my left to her right and back again as the hug turns into a kiss and then more.

"Reggie, I have a bedroom down the hall for the night, want to...?" We walk down the hall, taking a left into a bedroom. It is not one of the kid's bedrooms that is made over for aunties' stay. We sit uncomfortably on the edge of the bed. She takes me in and whispers with her mouth cupping up my ear, "I just don't want Michelle to hear me fucking and I have no idea how long baseball games last." I use my shoeless foot to peel the heel of my left shoe off. I roll her on her back, and she takes her earrings off and places them on a coaster on her nightstand. I don't know why this is a turn-on, but it is.

Goddamn, I wish we didn't have to rush, but there is added tension and excitement that is only tempered by the scratching and whining of a dog named Pepper on the other side of the door. "Piss off, Pepper!" Mika yells as we tumble.

-=-=-=-=-=-=-=-=-

Her sister's place. A drink and a meal and some back porch smoke by her and her sister after the kids go to sleep, and Peter excuses himself. I joke with Mika as I leave "Pepper and Peter, I don't know if it would be weirder if both of the kid's names started with a P or if it is weird that only Peter and Pepper's names start with a P." She laughs, hugs me, but this is a goodbye hug. It was only momentary; her body tells me that. The novelty of me had already worn off after just a few evenings.

"Take care, Reggie, thanks again for everything." I don't even know how I got home when I arrive. I unlock the front door, throw on the entry light and then lock the door behind me, shut off the light.

-=-=-=-=-=-=-=-=-=

I pull up to a curb of boxes, folding chairs, a vacuum...pink trash bags. It is the saddest parade float you might ever see. "You can go through it if you want to Marco, I am donating all of it to the veterans otherwise." Louise has her hair tied back, tennis shoes on, and a broom she is sort of resting on in her right hand. I don't want to go through his things. I don't even want these writings, but she insisted that I pick them up as they were specifically left in his will to me. "That asshole landlord was giving me grief about loading all of this stuff in front of the complex, but that is what the Veteran's told me to do when I called them. Leave it all in the front. They are coming on Wednesday." If she is grieving, she is not showing it. She is also not seeing it on me.

"I have that box of his writings that I will get out of the apartment for you, give me a sec." A few minutes later she pushes through the gated entryway with her two arms outstretched like a forklift. She is holding a box that once held reams of blank printer paper and has seen its better days. I grab it from the bottom, before the whole of the box gives way. Sliding it into the backseat, she watches me as if trying to sort if I have what it takes to care for Jerry's scribbles and doodles. "He always said he was going to write a book, maybe you and your friends can piece it together from that." It is not a question; it is a statement that she is making with her hand over her brow and one eye closed from the glare of the sun as she studies my face. I mumble something like a laugh and a "maybe" simultaneously while trying to be respectful.

I tell Louise to call me if she needs help with anything. "There is nothing else to help with," she says in a throaty rasp. "You have his life's work. I kept some photos and am giving the car to my nephew," she tells me real matter of fact. His life's work, as if Jerry's rambling journals are the queen jewel that I am unfairly taking from the family. I am only here as a favor. I don't want to be here. To see his things kicked curbside, his sister who has no inkling of who her brother even was. It is one of those conversations that you have with someone where you are both talking to someone else.

His life's work slides from left to right in the backseat as I take a quick right onto Third. It is going home with me right now, but I know that I won't be able to bring myself to look at it, nor bear to throw it out. Life's work. It will end up in storage, in the hands of strangers that don't value it. No one wants it. Any of our life's work.

32 Red

Have you ever known a winning gambler? One that walked out of the casino with a fresh kill of green and never went back in to lose? No quarter, not even a cent of them winnings, back into that stream again. Sure, you, maybe your pals have left winners, but most of you will be back to surrender with interest on top soon enough. I am speaking of a gambler that hit that pie in the sky and never played a hand again. I am that never again man, but that still doesn't mean that I won.

I sat at the bar in the 10 am hour, nursing a 7 & 7 at My Father's Place. There is a bar in nearly every major metropolitan town with that name. I have been to two, maybe three of them on my travels this year alone and it is only March sixteenth. They aren't a chain, they are all a bunch of related Ma & Pop, or sons and daughters running the joints, but none the same and all unrelated. They are like The Dew Drop Inn or Joe's Diner. There are scads of them. Most of the Joe's that birthed them are long gone but their namesake lives on for weary travelers or loyal locals that push those dirty doors open daily. I know the owner of this particular My Father's Place, Helen. She bought it from the previous owner and liked the name enough to keep it. She told me one morning a few months in "Do you know how much it costs to rebrand a dive?" laughing.

Helen is the short-order cook and the bartender in the mornings and five out of seven afternoons. I don't go to the place in the eve, too much riff-raff, too many drunks that haven't the ability to have just one. Just one 7 & 7, now and again, with my breakfast does me fine.

There is a group of my peers that gather outside the local bakery, nursing their coffees and making allowances for one another's shortcomings, but that circle is impenetrable by me. How could I join? What would I say anyway? Nah, I have spent years here. I don't want to tell my stories again. I good morning or good afternoon them outside of Tigerlily's Bakery, that is enough for me. I don't long to speak unnecessarily.

This minor stretch of a town off of the 395 was a godsend. I think it musta been built for me as a way to get out of Reno. To get far enough away from the folks that I knew there, but close enough to get back if I ever needed to. A funeral. An itch. I was near enough to drive my way back. Everyone I knew in town, in time, knew about my windfall. There was the photo of me with an oversized check. The casino broadcast to sucker in others thinking they would be that one in a millionaire. That one, a millionaire.

All the cliches came to visit me. Even the old friends that asked for nothing, wanted not for it, well they changed a little and I changed just enough so that our friendship was never the same.

Our small pond stardom means nothing in the desert, just a highway stretch from wherever we are. I am just another retired local here. That is exactly what I am, too. The desert unclothes all, at least our appearance for a spell.

"You want some coffee, maybe a side of toast to ring that

morning buzz out of your belly?" Helen says, swinging the pot mid-sentence.

"That got killed by the hash browns and ham, but sure, another cup, Helen. Thank you."

It is true. I did overdo it last night. Last night my son Steven would have been thirty-eight. We had a falling out and a few years later he was struck on the way home from work, left for dead by a motorist that they never did find. His sister phoned me. I was not a terrible father to either one of them, but absent. Absent even most of the time that I was there. Oh, that is the thing about joining any of these social scenes or making new friends. I don't want to talk about all of my failures. "How is your family?" is a question Helen has never asked me. I don't need to be told by newly minted former strangers about what a lucky guy I was. Asked "What did you do with the money?" asked "And you are still working?"

I am working every afternoon until eve. I toil in the workspace behind the house on old junk Chevies. Old junk caddies. I puzzle with them and they fuck with me. We troubleshoot together. Machines of all sizes, all of the troubles that have been allowed to passenger into them. They are my big metal crossword puzzles. My Jeopardy. This minor thing was known by Helen.

A few years back I switched out the alternator on her crappy old GEO. Maybe a $90 job at best, but gratis for her. It could have led to something, we both felt it, but nothing came of it. Well, endless cups of free coffee until she is no longer tending, that is what she insisted I take as payment when I pushed her hand away with cash after I refused a check.

-=-=-=-=-=-=-

I was on the wheel, and I pushed most of my winnings onto 32 red. The damn thing spun and steered its slowdown to me. 32 red. The table erupted. Strangers at neighboring tables clapped, hooted, and raised their drinks. I was embarrassed then. I was beet fire blushing.

I had seen too many made-for-TV movies, so after sorting out the winnings, I left town that night and rented a room at the Motel 6 in Sparks. Drank some Jim Beam from a liquor store bag over an urn filled with rocks from the motel's ice machine. I was blindsided. What on earth was I going to do now? Good news is as hard to digest as bad. It is fraught with trapdoors. You gotta be careful. I gotta be careful I remember thinking then.

I attempted to make up in finance to my kids for the ghost that I had been. I paid off Stacey's mortgage. I sent Steven a check for the exact amount of that payment. She was ecstatic. He was not. We talked over the phone the night that he received the check. The check would never be cashed and I would never hear his voice again.

I tuck a twenty and five next to my plate for Helen when she is busy tending to Sam. He is a regular here. Keeps quiet, doesn't bother no one. "Did you see that Richard Jay put his house up for sale?" he is small talking Helen. Perfect moment, now is my chance. I pull my license, my Texaco credit card, and my ATM card out of my drugstore faux leather wallet. I will need these cards with me for the drive home, for the just in case breakdown on the highway in the latest monster of a Chevrolet I am fucking around with. I take them cards of identity and slide them into my upper shirt pocket.

Nonchalant, to my left and right, eyes with myself in the mirror next to the Ansel Adams and James Dean headline newsprint. My eyes are the only ones on me. Perfect.

It is only Helen here, no one else behind the bar until 4 or so, I retell myself. Only her. I loaded that wallet up with as many hundreds as I could get into the webbing and still be able to close it. One good shove and it lands fatherly. I see it on the fatigue mat behind the bar, lying in wait.

I am grateful to Sam who, for once, is on a real tear about something. I don't even have to say goodbye to her today as she is sighing at his grievance. She is a barkeep. A cheap detective that learned on her feet. Be cautious, I told myself over and over. Were she to have looked at me for more than a moment earlier this morning, she would be able to see I was amiss, but I think I pulled it off as I head out the door.

"Jim," she calls out as I am pushing the AC onto the street with my failing body. Oh shit, oh no, keep walking. Act like you don't speak the language like when you are panhandled to death. Don't go back. But back I go. Go.

"This your wallet?"

I pause for what feels like a few minutes before walking further into My Father's Place. I am rosary repeating silently.

"Remember to be careful." Over and over again.

Be careful. Don't say anything. It is good to be called back. Not to plan, but this is a good chance to plant seeds. What have I done? My hands are in fists inside my pockets as I backtrack.

-=-=-=-=-=-=-

I was eighteen and had finally gotten that job at the movie theater I frequented weekly. My teen dream job. I was trained in by the manager on how to count out the till. Fifteen minutes after the last screening, I was brought into his office to count out and I was a couple bucks short. He told me to count out again, me at the far desk facing the wall, him on the phone as the count out mirrored the previous one. I pulled two ones out of my right front pocket and quietly slid them under the silver clasp without a bang of it landing.

"How am I supposed to trust you?" and "What the hell really happened tonight with your register?" boomed over my shoulders, him standing behind me. I know I jumped in my seat. My heart pumping extra beats.

He continued his lighting into me. "Was that your two bucks or my money you attempted to purloin and when caught, tried to sneak back in?" I only wanted to hold onto this job, at the cost of a couple of bucks to me, but this was even worse than just letting it all be. He let it slide, he said something like that followed by a terse "Keeping my eye on you, Jim boy." I continued working there for a few years and I came to believe that he and I would have had a strained working relationship no matter what, as every other employee there did in time.

-=-=-=-=-=-=-

I have crossed the threshold and back into the arms of My Father's Place. I am million miles a minute thinking, but every thought was now heading to the same conclusion. "Jim, is this your wallet?" Helen says again as I near. I am going to blow it again.

Tears well up in my eyes, to her I can't lie. She lifts the bar flap and comes over to me, takes my hand, and puts the wallet in it. "It was Steven's birthday yesterday." I slump and pull into my side. I am looking at her as closely as I have ever looked at anything. I turn her palm skyward out of mine, out of mine with the wallet, and I put the wallet in her palm, my hand on top. I try to eke out a "please" but it sounds more like a moan, a plea in any language. She is looking at me, looking at me without wincing. I hope for once, I can walk out the door a winner.

Richard and Manuel in The Hall of The Mountain King

For the most part, it was an incongruent marriage. A nasal reedy thing that was made even more annoying by the low-end mumble from beneath his nose. When broadcast on the phone, or the few times he was on a microphone, there was a third layer to get through, his odd mouth breathing that wool-sanded the receiving end of the phone or mic, where every "sh" or "th" obfuscated the next syllable out. The art of translating what he was saying was second nature to me, something I didn't have to work at. He was the rare childhood friend that had made it to adulthood with me. He was one of two. The other being his brother Richard. So just five seconds into picking up the phone, I knew something very good or the polar opposition of that was about to be communicated to me as Manuel's first words on the line were pitched up in a high register, not the voice of when he and I were kids, but that same over-excited sensibility.

"I just got back from Richard's. When I got to his door, I heard piano playing, Richard's piano playing through the door!" he started.

"It wasn't for show, as I arrived unannounced," of course, it was like that these days as Richard seldom picked up the phone and would not open the door were someone to knock, unless that knocking got insistent with your voice IDing who you were. At least that had been my experience the last few years of visiting him. Manuel, as his older brother's caretaker now, had the key to get in on weekly drop-offs or pop-ins or mop-ups. He continued.

"When I walked in, he was above it, concentrating and in the throes of his own playing. Larry, it was unbelievable."

Larry was a play on Lara from childhood. No one called me that anymore except Manuel. Richard used to call me that as well, but I don't recall him addressing me by name in the last decade or so. We are both feasting on this piece of good news. I am tough-minded, but Manuel, his voice could bring me to tears fairly easily in this or the lower rent cousin of his histrionics in this key. I was not crying. I had just woken up at close to four PM on that Sunday and was slow on the draw. It would take me a minute or two to shake awake. Manuel continued going on about the small details. He was too excited as yet to pause, but when he did, I got in the first question that was on my mind upon hearing this.

"What was he playing?"

What was he playing would be a tell. A tell to me, maybe Manuel. For Richard, there was a weight in the small things. He was always communicating. You just had to listen or look a bit closer at the context of everything. His body language, his intonations. It was exhausting trying to figure him out. I stopped, to a large extent. Too many brick walls. Too much reaching for nothing more than sheer.

"Grieg, fucking Grieg!" Manuel says singingly.

Grieg meant something to Manuel, me, and Richard. Grieg was a romantic, had a direct bloodline to Glenn Gould, had a moral compass, and suffered through a number of illnesses and emotional losses which he overcame to a miraculous extent, so much as anyone can, over the course of their life. Richard's choice of Grieg, now, was secondary to the fact that Richard was playing the piano again. Once more.

"...yeah, and he continued to play as I opened the door and took a seat on the living room sofa across from him. He played for twenty minutes Lara, and he sounded so good. Who knows how long he had been playing before I arrived? He looked like himself as he played. So good!"

He must have repeated the above in a few different lights as it had been at least ten minutes that we had been on the phone. I started to drift for a minute back to him saying those three words: "Grieg, fucking Grieg!"

Had anyone ever said those three words in tandem before?

-=-=-=-=-=-=-=-

Manuel was two years Richard's junior, and his only sibling. The two of them grew up in Ontario, California, just north of the airport with their backyard facing out to the main artery to the airport, Vineyard Ave.

My mother and I lived three houses down the street from them when the three of us were kids. Save for the Tomlinson's kids, who were in the same age bracket as the three of us, there were no other real kids on the block. We had our faults, but the Tomlinsons were, and I imagine if still living, the kind of strangers you want to keep that way. The popping-off jerk in line behind you at the movie theater, the dense rube that you may have been stuck with as a relative. No need to squint to define who they were. The Espinosa brothers and I played in the house and in our backyards. Better to be penned in than to be subject to them.

There was a brief moment in high school when the brothers and I were all in the same band class, but otherwise, the only crossover was after-school dreaming and long summers of TV or rummaging, scavenging, and searching for escape. My dad picked me up on the weekends, so I missed out on all of the adventures the brothers would have, or not have depending on the weekend. Dad's house was a bore. A series of kids from girlfriends he was dating, but I didn't like one of them. Their tastes and mine didn't meet up on anything.

Manuel and I got teased a lot, being of the same grade and being friends in elementary school and junior high.

"You love him, don't you?" A stupid seven-year-old Maryann Estes would tease. It would only get crueler and more pointed as our class aged into its teens.

"Manuel loves the owl girl. Manuel loves the owl girl." A chant around him one recess in fifth grade.

That brand of harassment lost its edge and subsided in high school when each of us was bullied for unique attributes that were ours alone, much of it divided by gender lines. Manuel's lisp and overgrown lanky body that couldn't hold any weight no matter how much he ate; my coke bottle glasses and poor clothing decisions did not aid me from any of the elements that appeared on our high school campus.

Richard though, he was touched. Being two years older than us, we didn't see as much of one another during our school days, but I know he was not teased, or bullied in any substantial way. He told the two of us as much.

"I don't know, I just get along with everyone for the most part," he offered as useless advice to Manuel and me. Every school has someone like Richard. A person that bothers no one. A kid that is not popular nor unpopular. This did not impress Manuel and me at the time. We wanted him either brought down to our level or to offer some kind of game plan on how to avoid being put upon. I suppose one piece of advice he could have offered to each of us was to drop out of band where I played the clarinet and Manuel the tuba. Are there two other instruments that scream *Hey, you, please beat me up* more so than those?

-=-=-=-=-=-=-=

Richard turned us on to classical music with visceral films that the three of us watched over and over again when he was a junior and we were both freshmen at OHS. *Five Easy Pieces, A Clockwork Orange,* and fittingly *Moonrise Kingdom* were our road in, each with a starkly contrasting soundtrack and tone both musically and visually. It was a triptych that became a talisman for the three of us. I owned all three on DVD in time to bookend the copies that the two of them had. Rainy day after school? Summer day no school? It didn't matter, we were latchkey kids watching one or the other of those films most days for a good stretch until I split right around five before my mom got home from work.

Far from those school days, I recall us discussing which of the three films could be ascribed to each of us. It was a settled affair rather briefly. Richard was *Five Easy Pieces* what with his Jack Nicholson charm that you could see turn into brooding if you knew to define that in him. I was *A Clockwork Orange* with my antisocial and misanthropic world view and of course, Manuel was *Moonrise Kingdom*. Optimism, playfulness, attention to detail, and the devil may care attitude of his.

It was not as if we didn't listen to Kendrick Lamar or Radiohead or other music of our time, but it was a quest to impress one another with pieces of another era that no one, except maybe the drama teacher and the librarian at our school, listened to.

"Stravinsky's *Firebird*, do you know that story?" Richard, calmly storytelling the riot that occurred during the premier of the piece. He had some of the details wrong. Maybe for added dramatic effect, which colored the whole piece when I pulled it up on my phone the first time that I heard it.

A week or so later was my turn, and I thought I had a good one.

"Charles Ives," I shot out like a cannon precociously and nearly taking cover for fear one of the bullies would fall out of a cloud and beat on me right then and there in the backyard of the brother's home. That beating, I reflect now, would have been understandable. Fourteen-year Charles Ives name dropper? It certainly wasn't my first overreach. I continued:

"He brought dissonance into the language of music," I said this without truly knowing if it was factual, but knowing I had read this and tried to hear it in a piece by him. I don't know if this meant anything to Richard. He was nonplussed then and didn't say a word. He didn't bring it up the following day as I had hoped he would nor any day thereafter.

Richard beat us at this game hands down. I was simply trying to impress him, obsequiously. He was buying second-hand LPs and CDs by classical composers and musicians for near nothing at the time at thrift stores and used record stores. I was pulling everything up on my phone or computer. How could I pretend to be as invested as him? Plus, two years is a lifetime between a fourteen- and sixteen-year-old in most instances. It was a lifetime for me to get to him anyway.

-=-=-=-=-=-=-=-

He came to answer the door that Manuel was beating on for what had been nearly ten minutes, unaware that it had been such a long march of thuds on the wood, car keys against the glass panes, and hollers of "Richard! Richard!" It was the last thirty seconds of this cacophony that stirred Richard out of bed and to the door.

"Hmm n..." Richard intoned to Manuel as he opened the door wide enough to let him into his apartment.

"Richard, are you okay?"

It was planned that the two of them would meet up this Saturday morning as Manuel's wife would be taking the two-year-old to her cousin's house today to catch up with some far-flung family that was of no interest to Manuel.

"You probably won't even see them again," Manuel had told Reet.

"I have only heard you mention them in passing in all of the eight years we have been together once, maybe twice," then he lied, "and besides, I have plans with Richard that Saturday."

Plans were then confirmed the following day via text between the brothers.

"Richard, are you hungover, sick? You should have called off." Manual isn't too concerned upon entry.

Oh my god, Manual thought, a minute in the door, "You are bleeding Richard. What is going on?" What looked like oil or dried paint was gluing most of the hair above Richard's right ear together, almost like a flap.

There was blood on his right top shoulder as well as caked blood on his neck, and ear. That was blood in his hair, too.

-=-=-=-=-=-=-

Twelve minutes into that call. "Lara, he was positively aglow. The playing was rough here and there, but his style was there and he pulled the piece from memory."

I went silent somewhere around there, silent to the degree that Manuel noticed.

"Larry, Larry... Lara?..."

I was remembering a visit the previous fall. Richard by now had reclaimed about as much of his mental faculties as his doctors had hoped he could. Hell, even exceeded them. But their expectations and those of his friends and family were not comparable. He then, at twenty-nine, said he felt like the mute father in a wheelchair, "In that film," he said, trying to place it, "that one film."

-=-=-=-=-=-=-

Manuel said he would pick me up, not to get a rental car. He was so above the clouds when I made my reservation. I was hoping to get there and in short order have my skepticism proven wrong. Get up that hill by will and look down at it all in wonder with him. Hoping. We had hoped in concert for years, or alone, solo in a car ride errand, first thing in the morning upon waking up. Even then, there was only so much disbelief that either of us could afford to suspend.

I am met by Manuel as I exit the jetway. He helps me load and unload my lone suitcase, shoulder bag, and airplane slump in and out of his car and into the lobby of the hotel. Him looking older, and sounding less enthusiastic, leads me to believe that we are back in the land of wishing and hoping.

"I'll call you tomorrow and let you know how things are looking then," he says under his breath. "I have to run to pick up Reet but we will all meet up for breakfast before heading to Richard's tomorrow."

I sling the shoulder bag over the suitcase on rollers and push my way into the elevator. The sixth floor, I get to know your smell as I shuffle trying to find the card key. I leave my belongings in the entryway next to the closet, and throw my jacket on the bed. I want to call someone, but who? Burden who? Whom would that be anyway? I brush my finger down the skin of my phone's address book before placing the face of it upside down on the nightstand. There is a small kitchenette with a minor amount of silverware, a few pots and pans, a kettle. Does anyone ever cook in this room? Has anyone? I shuffle through the tea choices, put the stove on. I remove the saran wrap from one of the two glasses on the sink, fill it three-quarters to the top, and have one sip before the phone hums. I wander back to the bedside to look at the number on my phone, it is no one. I pace the bedroom for a spell before turning to the bed, pushing the pillows up against the headboard, then lying on my side, facing the window. I am reminded that I had been in the small kitchen by the teapot's whistling. I can't, just yet, get up from the bed to still its calling. It will have to sing to itself for another moment or two as I listen in and stare.

Joyful and Triumphant

There were enough pillows on the queen-sized bed to suffocate a Sunday, she joked. There at the head, two oversized per side with a coupling of everyday use on both the hers and hers side. Then there were the throw pillows that Clabeth's mother had made for her when she was a child. One in the shape of a Turtle with a pattern of multicolored umbrellas hipside, upside and down with rainfall coming from every angle. Another was a rectangular pillow with a cartoon tuna fish sewn next to the cursive script that read *Even a fish wouldn't get caught if it kept its mouth shut.* I had ribbed Clabeth about that pillow years earlier.

"What in the hell drove your mom to make you that as a child?" the two of us laughing punch drunk for a quarter-hour.

"Dutch roots," Clabeth then, "Them hush hush Dutch mafioso roots!"

At the foot of the mattress was one of those plush dog beds that have a lip surrounding them. The accumulating Samoyed hair belonged to Perry who greeted us with tornado circles and tail slaps on the knees as we entered the foyer.

"Here," Clabeth motioned, pushing the dog bed to the floor, "You can change her here."

It had been a long morning, attempting to get everything into the car and everyone out of the house and then retrieving that which was most needed upon landing at Clabeth's house from out of the car. Luggage, books tucked beneath the armrest of the passenger side, the basket of toys, those could all wait until after dinner. Joyce in one arm and the duffel in my other with all of the wet wipes and the sippy cup and the balms and salves and potions to cure the worst of nine-month-old temperaments.

"Perfect," I say, laying Joyce down and pulling out a diaper. I can see that the side pocket which usually houses plastic bags looks to be empty, I dig around, taking the zippers tether to the opposing side. Nope, no former bag of granny smiths to be found here. "J, do you happen to have a plastic bag I can put the dirty in?" I have laid Joyce's changing blanket on top of the bed, scooted her onto it, and have my hand resting on her stomach. Clabeth leaning on the door frame gets pulled out of her gaze, "Sure, sure, one second," as she scurries to the kitchen cabinet.

Joyce is humming sing song as I change her. I think about how much waste I have created, am creating, and how much more I am asking the curve of the world to passenger for my children, grandchildren, and so on until the cycle ends. It is a huge ask, not of Clabeth, but of this ship we are all seesawing on.

There is a skylight that is not quite centered with the bed, but where Joyce is positioned, it is almost directly overhead. The sun is almost dead center above us as we are just inches from noon. I once had a skylight that leaked incessantly no matter how much caulking or grout or Plaster of Paris or quick set the landlord used to attempt to seal it. It was my first rental by myself, without roommates. It was heavenly, especially in the spring. The sun and moon landed dead center in the skylight during the spring in that living room. On cold April days, my cat would track the warmth coming in as she lay on the cherrywood floor.

Stretching to it, regal in the natural light. I finally stopped calling in for help after the landlord, in exasperation, said she would simply reroof the area if the latest fix did not take. It, of course, did not, so a throw rug and pots and pans as needed collected rain until I packed them with me for my move out of state.

"Here you are," Clabeth kneels bedside to get closer to Joyce and get the bag to me. Joyce curls her hand around Clabeth's finger. These are the moments we travel for. These minor notes.

There is a wave of laughter and unintelligible words making their way through the hall from the den and into the bedroom as we finish up. Clabeth has taken the baby in her arms. Maggie and Dwight and Maria are gathered on the front sofas. I sit cross-legged on the floor next to the end table as Clabeth returns to what I imagine was her spot with Joyce.

Joyce becomes center stage. I used to cringe when I would hear the carol "O Come, All Ye Faithful" during the holidays. But right now, I am reminded of it. The point in the song when the choir sings the line *Come let us adore him* specifically. That line, that goddamn line always struck me as vampiric, creepy. Goosebumps for the wrong reasons every time that song was playing overhead (never neck length, not eyeshot level in the car or on my home stereo either, no, always heard in a public place piped in from a wall at least eight feet high, a speaker pinching the ceiling or some other heavenly Muzak muscle to the north of me). It takes me until now, well into my forties, to get it and see it, what that lyric is attempting to voice. Attempting to sing. This, right here, in this room, is the rewrite, the final draft. Joyful and triumphant.

I lean back on my elbows and stretch my legs. Joyce points, "poppuh" and the room erupts into the warm kind of laughter that is akin to heat from a radiator. You know, not the flown-in vented stuff, but the hot-to-the-touch real thing right in front of you and in arms reach, not rat racing out from a maze in the heavens of the house.

It is quiet here, in the front room just a moment later. No one wants to direct nor influence what will come next from Joyce, from Perry as he sniffs around the baby blanket draped over Clabeth's arm. I push back at the windows of my mind. I lock the door and pull the drapes. Here, where the silence is absolutely breathtaking, nothing else shall be allowed in by any of us. For just a moment, not a note.

Lost Reflection

I caught it
In your hand-held mirror
The one in the upper left bathroom drawer
as It flew just out of sight from me
Was it a neighbor at the door?
The kids in the front yard rushing into the street after a tennis ball?
I rushed and I hurried and I was hasty
I shoved it in my left side back pocket
Threw the fire off of the stove
The mail into a rental check
And holy hell, I thought when I was done
I must no longer be young
For It tired me out
It tired me out
And I forgot
Until sitting down
About the reflection in my pocket
Cracking before being entirely lost to me

BAMBOO DART PRESS

112 N. Harvard Ave. #65
Claremont, CA 91711

chapbooks@bamboodartpress.com
www.bamboodartpress.com

www.ingramcontent.com/pod-product-compliance
Lightning Source LLC
Chambersburg PA
CBHW082227140626
46556CB00020B/3382